5-Minute
Treasury

pi
kids ®

An imprint of Phoenix International Publications, Inc.
Chicago • London • New York • Hamburg • Mexico City • Sydney

Published by PI Kids, an imprint of Phoenix International Publications, Inc.
8501 West Higgins Road   34 Seymour Street   Heimhuder Straße 81
Chicago, Illinois 60631   London W1H 7JE   20148 Hamburg

PI Kids is a trademark of Phoenix International Publications, Inc., and is registered in the United States.

www.pikidsmedia.com

ISBN: 978-1-5037-6002-8

Stories

Louie Likes Basketball
A STORY ABOUT SHARING

Huey, Dewey, and Louie are busy looking for Louie's missing basketball.

"Found it!" says Dewey.

"**Great!** I want to practice **dribbling**," says Huey.

"I want to shoot baskets," says Dewey.

"Wait a minute," says Louie. "Uncle Donald bought this for my birthday. That makes it **my basketball**! I'm the only one who gets to use it."

"I have an idea," says Huey. "We'll have a shooting contest. Whoever wins gets to play with the basketball."
"Good idea!" says Dewey.

"OK," says Louie. "But I know
that basketball is mine."
"I'll be the ref," says Donald.
Huey shoots first.
He makes **one** basket,
then **two** baskets,
then **three** baskets!

Dewey shoots next.
He makes **one** basket,
then **two** baskets,
then **three** baskets!

"So far, it's even,"
says Donald.
It's Louie's turn.
He makes **one** basket,
then **two** baskets...

SWOOSH!

...but before making his third shot, Louie says, "I have a better idea. I'll just keep the basketball! Thanks, guys!"
Then he

BOUNCE BOUNCE BOUNCES

the basketball down the driveway.

Huey shouts,
"Hey! Come back here!"

Dewey stomps his foot and says,
"Give us that ball!"

Donald says, "Not so fast! If you three can figure out a way to earn some money, then you can buy **two more basketballs**!"

"**OK!**" the boys shout. "**You're on!**"

But first they have to come up with a plan. Should they **mow lawns**? **Wash cars**? **Walk dogs**? Finally, they decide to open a **lemonade stand**!

Mickey and Goofy stop by for lunch.

"I brought us a sandwich **we can share**," says Goofy.

"How can we share **one** sandwich?" asks Louie.

"It's easy," says Goofy, "when the sandwich is

four feet loooong!"

The boys tell Mickey and Goofy about their plan to open a lemonade stand. Now Mickey has an idea. "We're making cookies this afternoon.

We can share them with you to sell at your lemonade stand."

"**Wow, thanks!**" says Louie. "You betcha!" says Goofy.

"YUM!"

When the cookies are ready,
Donald and Goofy do the dishes.
Mickey mops the floor.
"When we **Share the work**,
cleanup is easy!" says Mickey.

OOops!

Blub
Blub
Blub

"You know," says Huey, "this **sharing** thing kind of makes sense. That sandwich was yummy."

"And now we have cookies to sell with our lemonade!" Dewey says.

LEMONADE AND COOKIES FOR SALE

The boys agree to **share the work** for the lemonade stand. Huey makes the sign, Dewey makes the lemonade, and Louie calls for customers.

"Lemonade and cookies for sale!

Step right up!"

At the end of the day, the brothers count the money they made.

"Good job, fellas!"

says Donald. "You made enough to buy **lots** of basketballs."

"Hey…instead of buying more basketballs, what if we **share** this one? Then we can buy other stuff we want!" says Louie.

"I'd like to get a football!"

"Great idea!" says Dewey.

"I'll get a baseball and a mitt!"

"I'll get a soccer ball!"
says Huey.

"And we can **share** them all!" says Louie.

At the store, the boys pick out their purchases. They even buy some **tennis balls** for their Uncle Donald!

SPORTING GOODS

"Sharing works pretty well, don't you think?" asks Donald.

"You can say that again, Uncle Donald!" the nephews shout.

"Sharing is the name of the game!"

First Day of School

Morty is worried about the first day of school. He doesn't want to get out of bed. "What if the teacher is scary? What if no one sits with me at lunch? What if I have to go to the bathroom?"

"YIKES!" says Ferdie. "You sure have a lot of questions. We better go talk to Uncle Mickey."

"Hi-ya, Morty, hi-ya, Ferdie!" says Mickey. "Are you ready for your first day of school?"

Morty smiles, and then looks away. Mickey understands how his nephew is feeling.

DING-DONG!

"I invited some friends over to help!" says Mickey.

"What if no one sits with me at lunchtime?" Morty asks Minnie. "You can sit down next to someone," says Minnie. "Say hi, and tell them you like their lunch box. Now, let's fill up yours!" Morty packs a sandwich and an apple.

"What if the teacher asks me a question?" Morty asks.

"Let's practice," says Goofy. "A – B – C – D – E. What comes next?"

"F for Ferdie!" says Morty. "And then G for Goofy!"

"Gawrsh, you're smart," says Goofy. "I bet you're smart enough to go outside and wait for your Uncle Mickey!"

ABC
DE

What will I do at recess? Morty wonders, dribbling his soccer ball.

Then—SURPRISE!—Pluto runs over to Morty and noses the soccer ball. Morty smiles, and he kicks the ball back to Pluto.

"Great idea, Pluto," says Morty. "I'll ask someone to play soccer with me!"

It's time to go! Mickey brings Morty
and Ferdie to school.

"**WELCOME!**" says their teacher, Ms. Clarabelle, with
a great big smile. "Come on in!"

Morty peeks inside the classroom and sees...
a reading nook, art supplies, maps, a science center, toys,
a fish tank, a bathroom, and lots of friends, too!

"Wow!" says Morty. "I like school!"

"Good Morning, Millie and Melody,"

Minnie calls cheerfully. "Time for breakfast."

Minnie's nieces hurry to the table for their favorite meal of the day.

"I'll have some Toasted Crispy Coconut Curlies, please," says Melody.

"Me too!" says Millie.

"Oh, dear," says Minnie.
"There's only enough cereal for one.
Or you two could
Share what's left."

"**No,**" says Millie. "I'll have the cereal this morning because Melody had it yesterday."

"**No fair!**" says Melody. She holds on tightly to the box and…

OOps!

After breakfast, the girls get ready for school.
"I'm taking the yellow backpack today," says Melody.
Millie grabs the strap.

"It's my turn to take it," says Melody.

TUG!

"But it goes better with **my dress.**"

TUG!

"Hurry!" calls Minnie.
"The school bus is here!"
"Oh, just take it," says Millie.
"I don't want to be late."

At school, Melody chooses to do the
Colorful Carnations science experiment.

"I can't wait to see the white flowers change **colors**!" she says.

"That's what I was going to do," says Millie.

"But I remembered to bring the **food coloring**," says Melody. "It's right here in my backpack."

"You mean **MY** backpack!" says Millie.

POOF!

Ms. Clarabelle comes by. **"There's no need to argue,"** she says. "We have **So many** science experiments to choose from."

The
Exploding Volcano
experiment!

The
Floating Egg
experiment!

The
Disappearing Coin
experiment!

The
Sprouting Beans
experiment!

"**Ooh, I'll choose the beans,**" says Millie. "I always wanted to grow a beanstalk!"
"**Me too,**" says Melody.

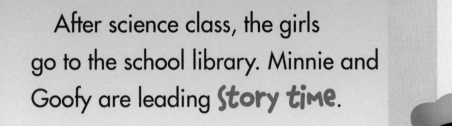

After science class, the girls go to the school library. Minnie and Goofy are leading **Story time**.

Plonk!

"What should we read?"
Goofy asks. **"Whoops!"**

Melody raises her hand. But before Goofy can call on her, Millie jumps up and shouts,

"Little Red Riding Hood!"

Melody frowns. "That's what I was going to say."

"Good," says Minnie. "You both like the same story."

"But it was my idea first!" says Melody.

"Can someone lend a hand?" asks Goofy.

At recess, the girls join their classmates for a jump-rope contest. Melody cuts in line to go first. Before the other girls can ask her to stop, she takes a turn.

JUMP!

JUMP!

JUMP!

"Melody," says Millie,
"you don't **play fair**."
"Well," Melody says,
"neither do you!"

Later, at the school festival, the girls compete for **a special prize**.

"I win!" says Millie. "I choose the teddy bear."

"I win too!" says Melody. "And I want the teddy bear."

"Oh, no," says Millie. "You should take a water bottle since you don't have one."
"No fair!" says Melody.

After the festival, everyone goes to the park.
Millie ignores the rules and cuts in line for the slide.

"No fair!" says Huey.

Melody ignores the rules and cuts in line for the climbing wall.
"No fair!" says Louie.

Then, Millie and Melody **both** cut in line for the swings.

"No fair!" says Morty.

When Millie and Melody finish playing on the swings, they look up and see that they are alone.

"Hey, where did everyone go?" Melody asks.

The girls find their friends on the soccer field.

"Why did you run off?" Millie asks.

"Because you and Melody were cutting in line and not taking turns," May explains. "If that's how you want to play…you can just play with each other!"

Millie and Melody look at each other. They want to play with everyone.

"We're sorry!" says Millie.

"We'll take turns from now on," Melody promises.

"That goes for us, too!"
Melody says to Millie.
"We can start by taking
turns with our things."
She hands her sister the
yellow backpack.

"And you can go first!"

Millie smiles and hands her
sister the teddy bear.

"And you can go first too!"

Both girls agree:
It's way more fun
to play fair!

Gilbert IS Not Afraid

A STORY ABOUT BRAVERY

"**Good mooorning, class,**" says Ms. Clarabelle.
"Next week, we're going on a field trip to the **Birch Canyon Nature Center!**"

All the students **cheer** ...except Gilbert.

OUR READING NOOK

I've never been on a field trip before! Gilly thinks.

When Gilly gets home from school, he tells his uncle Goofy the news.

"**Gawrsh, Gilly,**" says Goofy. "**Field trips are fun!**"

Gilly looks doubtful.

"You're going to see nature exhibits and all kinds of really neat, **creepy, crawly** reptiles!" Goofy adds. "Aren't you excited?"

"Sure…I'm excited," says Gilly, looking scared. "But it might **SNOW**. Then the trip **will be canceled**."

"**Huh?**" says Goofy. "You usually look on the bright side of things—where's that good ol' **Gilly cheer**?"

"Maybe I left it in my room!"

says Gilly,
and he runs off.

Goofy is confused.

Gilly is usually **curious** and **excited** about everything.
Could something be scaring him?

Gilly looks **worried** on Wednesday morning.
"Uh-oh," he says, "I lost the field trip permission slip.
Looks like I won't go after all."

"Have no fear! Ms. Clarabelle emailed it to me,"
says Goofy.

"Now, how about some fresh-squeezed juice?"

Gilly's classmates talk about the trip at school.

"We're going to **ride the bus**!" says April.

Bus? thinks Gilly. *But I ride with Uncle Goofy.*

"We're going to have Ms. Clarabelle's **cucumber** sandwiches!" says May.

Cucumbers?! thinks Gilly. *But I like Uncle Goofy's* ***humongous hoagies***!

Back home, Gilly helps Goofy
with yard work.

"Gawrsh, Gilly," says Goofy.
"That hole is **deep enough**.
Is something wrong?"

Gilly gulps. "I'm **afraid** to go on the field trip. What if I get **lost**?"

"Admitting you are afraid is **brave**!" says Goofy. "Now let's work on that **fear**."

splat!

Goofy runs to the bookcase and finds one of his favorite books, Flores Flamingo and the Fantastical Field Trip.

"See how Flores stays close to the other kids?" says Goofy.

"I can always find Flores in the picture because of her **colorful** shirt. Can I wear something **colorful** on my field trip, too?" asks Gilly.

"You betcha," says Goofy. **"I know just the shirt!"**

Later, Gilly and Goofy draw
animals that Gilly will see on the trip.

"What if the animals are scary?" asks Gilly.

"The nature center guide knows how to handle them and keep everyone safe," Goofy says. **"Let's hope the little critters aren't too scared of YOU!"**

Gilly laughs. He is feeling braver!

On the morning of the trip, Gilly puts
on his **Special Shirt** and goes outside to the
BIG yellow bus.

Honk honk!

"Let's moooove!" calls Ms. Clarabelle.
Gilly joins his friends and waves goodbye to Goofy.
He is feeling **BRAVE**!

Gilly **loves** the nature center! He is so curious and excited that he forgets he was afraid.

When the guide asks for a brave helper in the **chameleon corral**, Gilly raises his hand.

Hey, thinks Gilly, **I am brave**. I'm even ready to try *cucumber* sandwiches!

First Pet

Minnie has a **surprise** for Melody. "You get to pick out your first pet today!" she says.

Millie thinks her pet **HAMSTER**, Hubert, is perfect.

"But what kind of animal is best for me?" Melody wonders.

"Let's visit our friends' pets," says Minnie. "That will help you decide."

At Mickey's house, Morty and Ferdie are playing with their pet **DOG**.

"Scout loves to chase after things," says Morty.

"Fetch!" says Ferdie, and he tosses a ball. Scout **woofs** and **runs** after it!

"Such a playful pup!" says Melody.

Gilly has a pet LIZARD. "Her name is Rainbow," he says. "Her scaly skin can change color!"

"Millie would love to see Rainbow turn purple," says Melody. "But I like green best!"

A busy-buzzy fly flies by and…SNAP! goes the hungry lizard's loooooong tongue.

April, May, and June are feeding their pets. "Aunt Daisy says my **FISH** Bubble, Splish, Huck, and Samantha need just a *pinch* of fish flakes," says May.

April pours **crunchy kibble** into a bowl. "This is the *purrrrrfect* amount of food for my **CAT** Jubilee," she says. Melody looks around. "I'm ready to choose my pet," she says.

Now Melody has a **surprise** for Millie. "Guess what pet I chose," she says.

"Hmm…a skunk?" Millie guesses. "A donkey! Or…"

"No, silly!" says Melody. *"Change-o, presto—this pet's best-o!"*

A fuzzy **BUNNY** pops out of a hat! "Her name is Beatrix," says Melody. "She can do tricks, like Hubert!"

The sisters **love** their pets!

Huey, Dewey, and Louie are playing outside when Huey gets an idea. "Look at all those boxes in the garage," he says. "What if we had a **GARAGE SALE**? We could give the money to a local charity and clean out our stuff at the same time. It's a **WIN-WIN**!"

Huey's brothers want to help the community, too. But they don't want to have a garage sale.

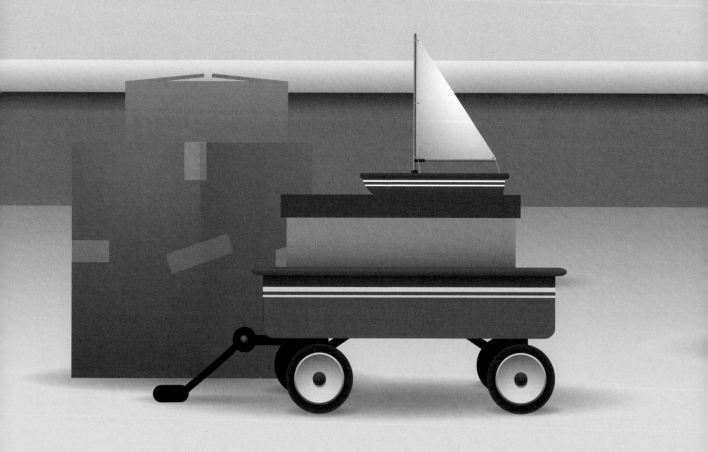

"Let's ask our friends what they think," Donald says to Huey. "I'm sure they'll want to pitch in and help when they hear your idea."

But Huey's friends all have **DIFFERENT** ideas about how to help.

"I think we should make **HERO SANDWICHES** for our **FIREFIGHTERS**," says Louie. "We can use Goofy's special recipe!"

"**HEROES** for the **HEROES!**" Goofy agrees.

Millie and Melody want to have a **BAKE SALE**.

"We'll give the money we make to the soup kitchen," says Melody. "They'll use it to feed families in need!"

"I can help!" says Mickey. "Everyone **LOVES** my chocolate chip cookies!"

But Huey would rather eat cookies than bake them.

"We can sell Mickey's cookies at a **LEMONADE STAND**," says Dewey.

"That sounds like fun!" adds Louie.

"Not as much fun as a garage sale," **GRUMBLES** Huey.

HMPH!

Gilbert has *another* idea. "We could ask stores to **DONATE TOYS** and then bring them to the children's hospital," he says.

"I know all the best toy stores in town," Goofy says with a laugh.

"Wait, I have an even better idea!" says Louie. "Why don't we have a **BASKETBALL SHOOTING CONTEST**? I bet lots of kids would enter. We can ask people to donate money for every basket we make. And we can use the money to buy equipment for the after-school sports program."

"That *could* be fun," Huey admits. **"But my idea is still the best!"**

"Hold on, boys," Donald says. "We've heard lots of good ideas. Let's ask everyone to **VOTE** on their favorite."

Huey's garage sale idea **gets ONE vote**, but the bake sale **WINS**.

Huey STOMPS his foot. "Go ahead and bake your cookies, but count me out," he says.

"I'M NOT HELPING."

"I guess we'll get started **without Huey**," Donald says. "Come on, everybody. We've got a lot of cookie baking to do!"

"And how about some pies, and tarts, and cinnamon rolls, too?" adds Goofy.

"I really  cinnamon rolls," says Donald.

Donald gets to work on the dough. *Extra yeast should make it rise extra fast,* he thinks.

The dough rises quickly...**AND IT DOESN'T STOP!**

Huey runs in with a shovel and says, **"I've got this!"**

When the dough is scooped up, the friends start
on the dishes. Working together, they get the kitchen

SPARKLING CLEAN.

"Can I still work the bake sale?" asks Huey. "I like helping. It makes me feel **happy**."

"You bet," says Donald. "I'm proud of you for pitching in."

Then, Millie runs in with *another* idea. "What if we do **everyone's idea**?" she asks.

Melody adds, "Huey can run the **GARAGE SALE**.

Goofy can make **HERO SANDWICHES**.

Gilly can hold a **TOY DRIVE**.

Dewey can set up a
LEMONADE STAND.

Louie can have a
BASKETBALL SHOOTING CONTEST.

And we can have
our **BAKE SALE**.
Think of all the people
we could help!"

"What do you think?" Dewey and Louie ask Huey.
"I LOVE it!" says Huey. "Turns out there are lots
of ways to help others and be kind."

YAY!

YIPPEE!

Everyone cheers! And everyone agrees:
you can't have too much kindness!

First Loose Tooth

Gilbert brushes his teeth twice a day, just like his Uncle Goofy.
Brushing keeps their teeth healthy and sparkly clean.

Then, one morning…

"Uncle Goofy, my tooth feels **wiggly**!" says Gilbert.

"Gawrsh, Gilly, it's your first loose tooth!" says Goofy.

"Pretty soon it will fall out, and a grown-up tooth will grow in!"

Each day, Gilbert's loose tooth gets **wigglier** and **wigglier**.

"Gee, Uncle Goofy, will it ever fall out?" he asks.

"Sure! But it might happen when you don't expect it, like when you're at school…"

CRUNCH!

"…or when you're having a snack!" says Gilbert. "Look, Uncle Goofy! My tooth came out!"

"Atta boy, Gilly!" says Uncle Goofy.

"I thought it might be scary, but it wasn't," says
Gilbert. He pokes his tongue into the gap. It feels funny!

"And now comes the best part," says Uncle Goofy.
"Before you go to sleep, put the tooth under your pillow.
The Tooth Fairy will take it and leave you a surprise!"

"Uncle Goofy, I can't wait until bedtime," says Gilbert. "Well, that's a first!" says Goofy. Gilbert makes signs pointing to his pillow—just in case the **Tooth Fairy** needs help. When he finally falls asleep, Gilbert dreams he can hear a pair of **fluttering** wings right outside his window...

As soon as Gilbert wakes up, he looks under his pillow.

"The Tooth Fairy came!" he shouts.

The tooth is gone. In its place is a pile of coins!

"...75, 80, 85, 90, 95..." Gilbert counts. "Whoa. Uncle Goofy, the Tooth Fairy left me a whole dollar!"

A few weeks later, Gilbert is helping his teddy bear brush his teeth.

"Hiya, Gilly!" says Uncle Goofy. "What's new?"

"My new tooth! It's starting to come in. See? It's here, next to the **wiggly** one!"

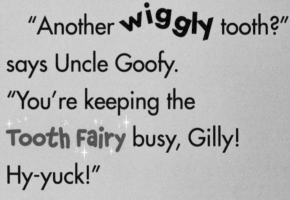

"Another **wiggly** tooth?" says Uncle Goofy. "You're keeping the **Tooth Fairy** busy, Gilly! Hy-yuck!"

Morty Tells the Truth
A STORY ABOUT HONESTY

Morty and Ferdie are having some fun playing with **sticky**, **icky goo**.

"We better put our backpacks and stuff away, so we don't make a **mess**," says Ferdie.

But Morty doesn't listen.

"Look at this, Ferdie!" shouts Morty.
"I made a volcano and it's about to erupt! **Run**!"
The **goo** spreads everywhere, just like lava! It seeps under Morty's backpack—and covers his **library book**.

Kaboom!

Uh-oh!

I can't let Ferdie see the **mess** I made of my *library book*, Morty thinks.

He quickly sits on the **goo**-covered book to hide it.

drip

drip

The next morning, Morty tells his Uncle Mickey that he can't find his **library book**.

"Have you seen it, Ferdie?" asks Mickey.

"Nope," says Ferdie.

"But **I'll help** you and Morty look."

Morty, Ferdie, and Mickey search through the toy chest and explore under the bed. They come up **empty-handed**.

"Time for school,"
says Mickey. "I'll keep
looking for your **book**."

"We were playing
outside last night," says Ferdie.
"Maybe it's out there."

While the boys are at school, Goofy comes over to help Mickey search.

"I don't see the **book** anywhere," says Mickey.

"We'll find it," says Goofy. "I'll **dig up every inch** of your backyard if I have to!"

At school, Morty tells his teacher that the **book** is lost. "Oh, dear," says Ms. Clarabelle. "I'm sure the class will help you look."

Morty's friends search their **classroom**,

the **art room**,

the **music room**, and the **playground**,

but no one can find the **book**.

When Morty gets home, Mickey can tell he is **sad**. "Guess you didn't find the **book** at school," Mickey says. "Goofy and I didn't find it here, either. But don't worry. Donald said he would come over and **help you look** some more."

sigh

Donald takes Morty to retrace all of his steps from yesterday. They walk to and from the school,

looking high...

...and low,

from the top of the slide to the bottom of the swing set. But still, no book.

The next day at school, Mr. Goodman the custodian finds Ferdie.

"I think this **book** belongs to your brother, Morty," he says. "His name is the last one on the library card."

drip

"Wow!" says Ferdie. "Where did you find it? We've been looking everywhere."

"I found it in the trash can by the playground," says Mr. Goodman.

When Ferdie sees Morty, he hands him the goo-covered book. "You'll never guess where this was found," says Ferdie.

drip

Squish

"In the trash can by the playground," says Morty, sighing sadly. **"I know...**

...because I'm the one who put it in there."

When the boys get home, Morty shows Mickey
the damaged **book**.

"Why did you lie to us?" asks Ferdie.

"I was afraid of getting in trouble for wrecking it," Morty explains. "So I threw it away and pretended it was lost. **I'm really sorry**."

"A lot of people helped you look for that **book**," says Mickey.

"I'm going to say **I'm sorry** to each of them," says Morty.

"And I'll use my allowance money to pay for a brand-new **book**."

"I'm proud of you for making the right decision," says Mickey. "You can never go wrong by being honest."

Morty agrees: **It's better to tell the truth!**

Millie Can Wait
A STORY ABOUT PATIENCE

WHEE!

Millie can't wait for Saturday! She's going to play outside **ALL DAY**. There are lots of things she wants to do...

ride her bike...

walk Fifi...

ARF!

...and jump rope.

SKIP! SKIP!

But when the day finally comes, it's

POURING
RAIN
OUTSIDE!

"Oh, no," says Millie, feeling disappointed.

"Why does it have to rain TODAY?"

"When will the rain ever stop?" Millie wonders. She looks at her bucket of colorful chalk. "Just as soon as the sidewalk dries, I'm going to draw a **RAINBOW**."

Meanwhile, Minnie and Melody are busy playing **GO FISH**.

"Why don't you play with us?" asks Minnie.

But Millie wants to be ready to go outside the minute the rain **STOPS**. "When do you think it will stop raining?" she asks.

"Hmm, I don't know," says Minnie. "I haven't checked the weather report."

Minnie lets Millie check the weather app on her phone. The app takes a long time to load, and Millie doesn't want to wait. She tries the TV, but there is just a bunch of fuzz on the screen because of the storm.

"Nothing is working!"

In the meantime, Minnie and Melody have finished their card game and started on a baking project.

"Don't you just love the smell of **FRESHLY BAKED COOKIES**?" asks Melody.

MMM!

"I'll be outside long before the cookies are done," Millie says. "But save me some."

Millie looks out the window. She looks away, and then looks again. It's still raining. **She's tired of waiting!**

Maybe I can stare the rain away, she thinks.

While the cookies cool, Minnie and Melody take
out a JIGSAW PUZZLE. Millie loves doing puzzles.

Millie walks over and watches. "It's taking you an awfully long time to finish that puzzle," she says. "It could go faster if you helped," says Melody.

"Oh, all right," Millie says. "But just for a few minutes!"

When the puzzle is done, Melody pulls out a stack of books. "Let's **READ** until the rain stops," she says.

"Maybe just a *short* book," says Millie. "I'm pretty sure the sun will come out any minute."

Soon, Millie is finished with her book. "That was really good," she says. She takes a quick look out the window. It's still raining—but this time, she doesn't mind. "Being inside isn't so bad," she says.

"What can we do next?"

Melody pulls out the **CHECKERS**. "You could have been **PLAYING GAMES** and **BAKING COOKIES** with Aunt Minnie and me this whole time," she says.

"You're right," says Millie. "This is **FUN**. Especially when I win!"

TEE-HEE!

"Remember that mural we always talked about painting in our bedroom?" asks Melody. "Let's do it!"

"Great idea!" Minnie says cheerfully. "I'd love to see something **COLORFUL** on that wall."

Just when Millie paints a cloud under her **RAINBOW**, it **STOPS** raining.

"You can finally go outside!" says Minnie.

"Now?!" says Millie. "But we're not finished."

GASP!

DRIP!

"You've wanted to play outside all day, Millie," says Minnie. "Now's your chance!"

Millie looks up and smiles.

"It's OK, Aunt Minnie," she says. **"I can wait."**

First Time Cooking

"**W**hat do you boys want for dinner?" Donald asks one night. Louie wants green salad, Dewey wants fruit salad, and Huey wants pasta.

"Yum, a three-course meal!" Donald says. "Want to help me cook it?"

We need more apples!

First, they go shopping.

"Can we get muffins?" Louie asks. "And a watermelon?"

"That sounds delicious," Donald says, "but let's stick to the list for tonight's dinner!"

The boys spot some friends in the produce aisle.

"Are you making dinner tonight too?" Louie asks.

"Yeah! We're having sandwiches," Gilbert says.

"And all my favorite fruit!" says Goofy.

BAKERY

At home, the kids unpack the groceries and get cooking!

"I'll peel carrots for my green salad," says Louie.

"I'll chop apples for my fruit salad," Dewey says.

"And I'll help stir my pasta!" Huey says.

The brothers stir, and peel, and chop...and stir, and peel, and chop...

"Oh!" Daisy says. "I think that's enough pasta. And carrots. And apples!"

Donald calls a few friends. "The boys helped me make dinner," he says. "But now we need help eating it!"

When the food is ready, Donald says, "Our guests will be here soon, boys! Could you please set the table?"

Help!

Soon, their friends arrive—with more food!

"We made mashed potatoes," Millie says.

"And three kinds of pie," says Melody.

"Gawrsh, we only made one sandwich!" Goofy says.

"That's OK," says Donald. "I think there's enough to share!"

After dinner, Huey says, "That was fun! And yummy!"
"I want to cook again tomorrow night," says Louie.
"I want to cook again every night!" Dewey says.
"That's great!" says Donald. "But first, let's clean up
the mess from tonight!"

June Gets a Job
A STORY ABOUT RESPONSIBILITY

June loves to give her Aunt Daisy's dog, Jewel, a **BATH**.
"You're doing such a good job," says Daisy.
"The secret is having **TREATS** in your pocket,"
June says with a **GIGGLE**.

ARF!

"How about a few customers?" asks Minnie. "Fifi could really use a bath."

"I'll wash her right now," says June.

"That goes for Pluto, too!" Mickey says.

"Hmm," says Daisy. "This sounds like the start of a little business."

June thinks this is a **GREAT** idea.

POP! POP!

"What do you think, Pluto?" June asks. Pluto answers with a loud

WOOF!

Soon, word of mouth reaches their neighbors and friends. Everyone wants an appointment for their pooch. June's new job **_TAKES OFF!_**

The next day, Jewel has an appointment for a **BATH**. As June gets the pup ready, her sisters April and May join them in the yard.

ARF!

"Don't forget we're having a picnic at noon today," says May.

"I'll be ready," replies June.

Just as June puts Jewel in the tub, a squirrel runs through the yard. **Jewel wants to play!** She **CHASES** after the squirrel, **RUNS** through the open fence, and **RACES** down the sidewalk.

SQUEAK!

ARF!

"Wait!" cries June. "I can't run as fast as you!"

WIGGLE! WIGGLE!

Jewel stops to sniff the ground, but as soon as June gets close, she **RUNS OFF AGAIN!**

June returns home just before noon, **without Jewel**.

"We have to leave right now!" says April. "Our friends are waiting for us."

June doesn't want to make her sisters late. But she doesn't know what to do about Jewel!

When June explains what happened, Daisy has an idea.

"I'll ask Donald, Mickey, and Minnie to help me look around the neighborhood for Jewel," she says. "You three go have your picnic."

SIGH!

At the park, the girls set out their picnic lunch. Soon, everyone is busy **LAUGHING** and **EATING**—**except June**.

"You're awfully quiet, June," says May.

HA!

HA!

CRUNCH!

CRUNCH!

June feels bad that she isn't helping Aunt Daisy.

"I'm going to look for Jewel at the pond," she says.

"That's her favorite spot!"

As June gets near the pond, she sees
Ms. Clarabelle with her three dogs, Cissy,
Chrissy, and Missy. **And she sees Jewel!**
The dogs **RUN** in circles, trying to chase
the geese. Ms. Clarabelle gets **TANGLED**
up in the leashes.

HONK!

HONK!

BARK!

HONK!

"Oh, dear," she says. "Can somebody please unwind me?"

June **HURRIES** over to help Ms. Clarabelle. She pulls some biscuits out of her pocket and tells the dogs to sit as she **UNTANGLES** the leashes.

"Thank goodness for **TREATS**!" says June, as she scoops up Jewel and gives her a hug.

SLURP!

Just then, Daisy and her friends arrive.

"You found Jewel!" says Daisy.

Jewel is panting and happy. She's **ROLLED** in so much **MUD** on her adventure, she's really dirty now!

"Looks like Jewel needs another bath," says Daisy.

"She's going to be *my first and last* customer of the day," says June.

"I'd like to hire you too," says Ms. Clarabelle. "I can see that you're **GREAT** with dogs."

"I'd be happy to wash Chrissy, Cissy, and Missy," says June. "But first, I need to get Jewel into the tub... **RIGHT AWAY**!"

BARK!

YIP!

WOOF!

Back home, June gives Jewel the **BEST BATH EVER.**

POP! POP!

"I'm really proud of you for taking your job so seriously," says Daisy. **"Being responsible is important to me,"** says June. "And I want everyone to know it!"

"ARF! ARF!" Jewel agrees.

Gilbert Tries Again
A STORY ABOUT PERSISTENCE

On a sunny afternoon, Goofy's nephew Gilbert comes **RACING** home from school.

"I've got an art project, Uncle Goofy!" he calls. "And it's due tomorrow."

"OH BOY!" says Goofy. "What's the project, Gilly?"

WHOOOSH!

"It can be anything. I could make a **MASK**, or a **PENCIL HOLDER**, or maybe a **PAPER-MACHE DOG**. But I've never made any of those things before," says Gilly.

"I DON'T want to MESS UP."

"You never know until you try," says Goofy. "I'll do the project with you!"

Goofy runs out of the room and comes back with artist smocks and berets. "What do you think about **painting** our own *PORTRAITS*?" he asks.

Gilbert begins painting his portrait. Then he steps back and looks at his work.

"This **DOESN'T** look like me *at all*," he says.

"This is NOT the right project."

DRIP!

"I think I'll try a **paper-mache** ANIMAL," Gilly decides.
Goofy and Gilbert cut newspaper strips and cover them in glue. Gilbert tries pasting the strips to a balloon, but they stick to his hands and shirt.

"This is FUN," says Goofy.

"This is a drippy, sticky MESS!" cries Gilly.

"Maybe we should check the directions in the craft book," says Goofy.

"I followed the directions. This doesn't look like any kind of animal. I'm **DONE** with paper-mache," says Gilly.

"AND THIS ART PROJECT!"

"Gawrsh, Gilly," says Goofy. "**Don't give up**.

Let's get cleaned up and try something else. How about **painting** a *LANDSCAPE*?"

"OK, I guess," says Gilly.

As they carry art supplies outside, Goofy accidentally trips and spills the paint all over the floor!

It pools into one yucky **brownish**, greenish, yellowish color that reminds Gilbert of a **STINKY, ICKY SWAMP**.

"I am DONE painting," he says.

"How about making **BALLOON** ANIMALS? I can teach you. I'm an expert!" declares Goofy.

Gilbert remembers Goofy making them at Huey, Dewey, and Louie's birthday party. They were a **BIG** hit!

"Watch closely," says Goofy.
He **blows up a BALLOON.**
"Now give it a little *twist* here and a little *turn* there, like so."

SQUEAK!
SQUEAK!

But when Gilly takes a turn, he

POPS

every single balloon.

He's ready to give up!

"Hold on," says Goofy. "Why don't we make something with this **CLAY**?"

"I guess I can try **one more time**," says Gilly.

He begins molding and shaping the clay. Suddenly, the clay begins to stiffen. Gilbert's hands are **STUCK**!

"Oh no," says Goofy. "This was *quick-drying* clay!"

Goofy grabs hold of the hardened clay and pulls. It comes off, but cracks in half!

"THAT'S IT!" cries Gilly. **"I GIVE UP!"**

"I don't want to make ANYTHING ELSE," says Gilbert.

"Nothing?" asks Goofy. "Not even a HOT FUDGE SUNDAE?"

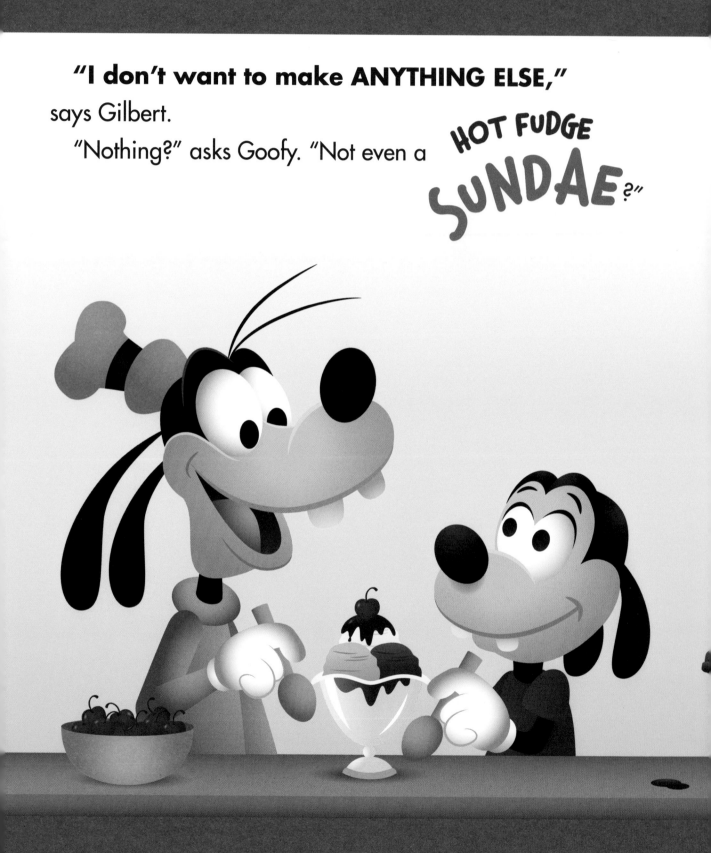

Gilbert and Goofy go to the kitchen
and make a sundae. It looks so good, Gilbert
decides to take a **picture**.

"Too bad THIS can't be my art project,"
Gilly says with a **GIGGLE**.

"It CAN be!" says Goofy. "The sundae, the photo, and all the things **you** made. They're all art, because they came from your **IMAGINATION**."

"They didn't all turn out how I imagined. But you know what?" says Gilly.

"I'm GLAD I NEVER gave up."

GILLY'S SUPER-TERRIFIC HOT FUDGE SUNDAE